Fizza the Flamingo

by Marilyn Sheffield

Illustrated by Patricia Al Fakhri

STACEY INTERNATIONAL, LONDON

The desert is very dry with little or no rainfall. It is full of sand. The sun shines most days.

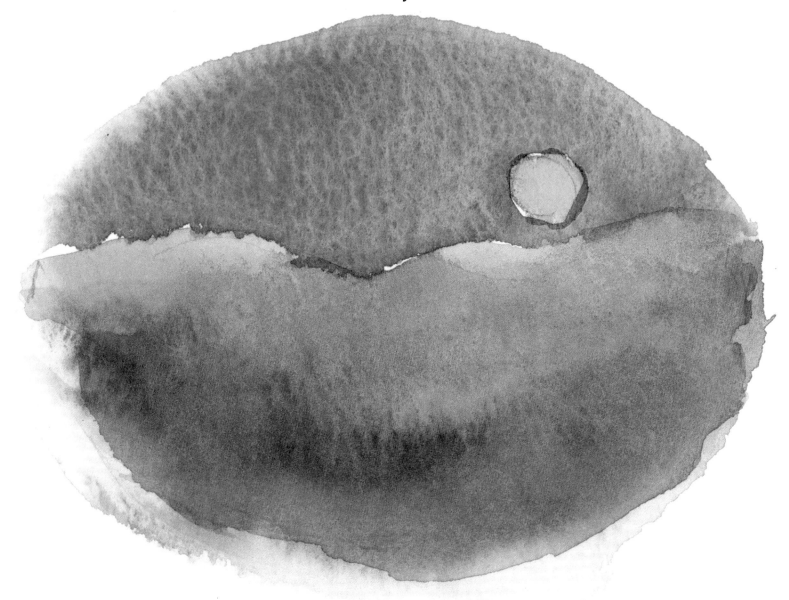

An oasis is a green place in the desert where trees
and plants grow. It is fed by underground water.

Fizza the flamingo lived in Dubai on the salt flats behind the huge skyscrapers of the Sheikh Zayed highway. Most days she saw the sunshine reflecting on the blue, green and pink glass of the skyscrapers. Every day she heard the noise of the traffic rumbling up and down the highway.

4

"What a noise!" she shrilled one day when she was trying to have a nap. "It's impossible to sleep," she grumbled to Mama Flamingo of the desert.
"I know, my dear. It is a nuisance, but we have to get used to it."

"We can fly off to nest in a more peaceful place in the summer," added Mama patiently. Fizza loved the lake in the valley far away, hidden among the purple mountains.

6

Fizza was cross. She was tired and grumpy because she could not sleep. She dipped her head into the salty water to freshen her face.

"This noise will make me quite deaf," she thought. I must get away for a while.

"Mama, I'm going flying," she called.

"Be careful and watch out for danger!" replied Mama.

"I will," she yelled as she climbed higher into the sky.

It was quieter and colder up in the air, near the clouds. She rested on the top of a thin wispy cloud. She wriggled about. "This cloud is not very comfortable. I must find a better one," she mumbled.

She hopped around until she found a cloud that was white, puffy and fluffy and very comfortable. "Mmmmmm, that's much better!" she sighed. Fizza snuggled down in the cotton wool cloud. She fell asleep in a minute, away from all the noise of the city. Fizza slept well.

She was in a good mood when she woke up. She saw the rows and rows of traffic down below. Big lorries, little vans, fast cars, new cars, old trucks, motor bikes, school buses, four wheel drives all going somewhere, weaving across the lanes and tooting their horns. "I think I'll fly into the desert. It is very quiet there. I don't want to go back so soon," she decided.

10

Fizza followed the cars towards Abu Dhabi until she came to the mountains of Hatta. She rested on an outcrop of rock and drank some sweet water from a rock pool filled from streams hidden deep in the mountains.

11

She watched a mouse hiding under an Oleander flower, growing wild in the wadi. "The flowers are beautiful but the Oleander is poisonous. That is a danger. I'll keep away from it," said Fizza to herself, remembering Mama's words.

12

Fizza could hear the noise of the date palm trees rustling in the breeze and the spring water from the mountain, gently cascading and splashing into the rock pools. "This oasis is wonderful," she said dreamily.

13

Fizza spread her pearly white wings
edged with cherry pink. She stretched her
long pink neck and long, long pink legs and
took off, showing some of her jet-black
feathers under her white wings.

Fizza landed on the soft red sand. She could see nothing of interest for miles and miles.

"I think this might be boring. There is no-one to play with and nothing to do. There is no shelter and I will burn in the sun," she thought.

Fizza saw three rocks. "Good, I might find another drink of water. The sun makes me very thirsty," she said.
One of the rocks, a black one, moved. Fizza jumped.
" Goodness me! A rock moving all on its own."
"I'm not a rock I'm Jamal the camel!" said the camel indignantly.
"I was sleeping. The other two rocks are my brother and mother. I'm black like my father who lives far away."

"Excuse me! I've never seen a black camel before," said Fizza.
"Are you a new one?" she added.
"I'm quite new but not a baby. I'm sort of a child, if you know what I mean," he replied.

The little black camel was woolly like a sheep, with black curls all over his body.

"Is there anything to eat out here in the desert?" Fizza asked him.

"For me, yes. I eat the thick gorse bushes," he replied.

"Ah well! I'll be on my way," said Fizza.

"Don't get lost in the desert, will you?" asked Jamal the camel.

"Don't worry, I won't," she said.

18

Fizza flew on, enjoying her trip out into the desert, away from all the noise of the city. She spotted a tree in the distance. "It's time I had another rest," she said to herself.

Fizza saw a desert gazelle under the big tree. "Don't be afraid. I'm Fizza the flamingo. I live near town and I don't eat deer!" Fizza said. She wanted to calm the frightened gazelle. "I won't hurt you," said Fizza gently.

Soon they were the
best of friends.

"I'm going further into the desert, to find another oasis," she boasted to the gazelle.

"Mind you don't get lost," said the gazelle, looking at Fizza with his black eyes shining like deep wells of oil.

"Me? Get lost? Never! I can fly back home any time I like," said Fizza.

Fizza flew on and arrived at the huge
sand dunes. The wind had swept the
sand high, making red hills with
patterns along the sides of the dunes.
Zigzags curved up the hills like snakes
squirming sideways across the desert.

The sun's
rays were very
very hot. Fizza
looked for the biggest
dune of them all. She
pretended that the hill was a
giant slide. Down and down she
slid. "This is great fun!" she giggled,
fluttering her wings to keep her balance.
    Fizza landed in a heap at the bottom. She flew
right back to the top and did it all again.
    "This is soooo good!" she screamed at the top of her voice.

She was dizzy from her game. She did not rest. She flew off again further into the desert. There was nothing but sand. She flew South. Only sand and more sand.

"Everywhere looks the same," she said, looking round.

"I must have flown in the wrong direction," she thought.

"Maybe if I try this way I will be nearly there." She flew off to the North and still couldn't find the oasis. Then she flew to the West and then to the East. She flew round and round in circles. Everywhere looked the same.

N

W.

E

S

"Oh no! I think I'm lost in the desert," she cried. "There is nobody about to ask the way. The desert is empty. If I fly too far I might get too hungry and weak. I will get sunburnt with the red-hot sun. What am I to do?" Fizza looked all around over and over again. She saw something black moving in the distance.

She flew off to see what it was. It was Jamal the camel
and his family heading for home.
Fizza landed right in front of them.
"Thank goodness it's you, Jamal the camel!
I'm lost in the desert and don't know
which way home is," said Fizza in a
fluster. "Everything looks the same
in the desert,"
she added.

"Camels have been wandering in the
desert for thousands of years. We know how
to get home," he replied.

27

"It's a good thing you are black
otherwise I would never have seen you," Fizza
said thankfully. "I shall follow your hoof prints in
the sand. Thank you for being in the desert and
saving my life."
She had no problem finding her way home,
following the foot prints in the sand, before the
wind blew them away.

She flew over the Sheikh
Zayed highway onto the salt flat
lake. "Whew, that was some trip!"
she said, glad to be home among her
family and friends. Next time she flew
off she would watch out for the
danger of getting lost. For the time
being she was glad to be home.
That is until the next time she
wanted a snooze!

Other children's titles by the same authors:

Elvis the Camel (Stacey International)   Barbara Devine
                                                Patricia Al Fakhri

The Pearl Diver (Stacey International)   Julia Johnson
                                                Patricia Al Fakhri

Oh No, The Pink Flamingo Turned Green! (Macmillan Caribbean)
                                                Marilyn Sheffield
                                                Katie McConnachie

Fizza the Flamingo

published by

Stacey International

128 Kensington Church Street

London W8 4BH

Tel: 020 7221 7166 Fax: 020 7792 9288

ISBN: 1 900988 631

CIP Data: A catalogue record for this book is available from the British Library

© Stacey International 2002

1 3 5 7 9 0 8 6 4 2

Design: Sam Crooks

Printing & Binding: Oriental Press, Dubai